Some crimes are more interesting than others.

Some killers are more surprising than others.

Today's murderer appears to be a crab.

# R.W. WALLACE
Author of the Ghost Detective Series

# CRITTERS

A Mystery Short Story

Critters

by R.W. Wallace

Copyright © 2019 by R.W. Wallace

Copy editing by Jinxie Gervasio
Cover by the author
Cover Illustration 67963427 © Elena Pimonova | 123rf.com

All characters and events in this book, other than those clearly in the public domain, are fictitious and any resemblance to real persons, living or dead, is purely coincidental.

All rights reserved. No part of this publication may be reproduced, distributed, or transmitted in any form or by any means, including photocopying, recording, or other electronic or mechanical methods, without the prior written permission of the publisher, except in the case of brief quotations embodied in critical reviews and certain other noncommercial uses permitted by copyright law. For permission requests, write to the publisher, addressed "Attention: Permissions Coordinator," at the address below.

www.rwwallace.com

ISBN: [979-10-95707-05-9]

Main category—Fiction
Other category—Mystery

First Edition

14 13 12 11 10 / 10 9 8 7 6 5 4 3 2 1

# Also by R.W. Wallace

## Mystery

### The Tolosa Mystery Series
*The Red Brick Haze* (free)
*The Red Brick Cellars*
*The Red Brick Basilica*

### Ghost Detective Shorts (coming soon)
*Just Desserts*
*Lost Friends*
*Family Bonds*
*Till Death*
*Common Ground*

### Short Stories
*Cold Blue Eternity*
*Hidden Horrors*
*Gertrude and the Trojan Horse*
*First Impressions*
*Let Them Eat Cake*
*Out of Sight*
*Two's Company*
*Like Mother Like Daughter*

## Science Fiction (short stories)
*The Vanguard*
*Quarantine*
*Common Enemies*

## Adventure (short stories)
*Size Matters*

## Fantasy (short stories)
*Unexpected Consequences*
*Morbier Impossible*
*A Second Chance*

At times, I've found myself…jealous, for lack of a better word… of my American counterparts. Those guys do the craziest crimes, making for the craziest headlines.

Like people stealing alligators from a zoo. Trying to rob a convenience store with a gun cut out of soap. Seriously, those guys manage anything.

Up until today, my oddest job was a drunk calling the police on himself for making too much noise one night.

Right now, I appear to be looking at a guy killed by a crab.

It's not as grotesque as it sounds—or at least, it's not grotesque in the way it sounds. The crab didn't cut his throat or anything.

It cut his toe.

Which, I assume, somehow made the victim fall off his balcony on the third floor and fall to his death on the city's busiest pedestrian street.

The crab's claw is still on the guy's big toe, but the rest of the animal has yet to be found. I've ordered one of my officers to look for it because it seems likely the crab was along for the fall but lost its claw on impact.

Yep, I gave that order.

I have seven officers on scene at the moment with more on the way. *Nordre gate*—meaning North Street in Norwegian—is *the* pedestrian street of Trondheim. It has shops, coffee shops, ice cream vendors, everything. Needless to say, on a Saturday offering an unusually blue sky on an August morning, it's crowded as hell, and people tend to be morbidly curious about a dead body. So at the moment, all my manpower is going into securing the scene, and—

"No pictures, please!" I yell at a blond guy in his twenties who's aiming for a selfie with the dead guy. I stalk over to push his arm down. "Show some respect," I tell him in my sternest voice. "You put that up on Instagram and I *will* come after you."

I won't, of course. Don't have the time for petty stuff like that. But this guy doesn't know that.

His eyes widen at the sight of my uniform towering above him and he scurries off, holding his phone to his chest with both hands.

Two colleagues manage to find the time to cover up the dead body with a tarp. Though it's not going to lessen the crowd's curiosity much, at least I don't have to worry about pictures of an ongoing investigation on social media.

I scan the crowd for any other over-enthusiastic photographers, but don't see any. There's a woman with two kids in tow—both below the age of ten—and I wonder what makes her think this is an appropriate occupation on a Saturday morning. Next to her, a guy is scratching his crotch—like, really scratching, making me wonder if I should take him in for public indecency—while his eyes are fixed on the spot where the dead body is hidden. Three young girls, probably high school age, have their heads together while whispering and pointing at the tarp. I can't hear what they're saying, but the giggles must be heard for miles around.

Shaking my head at the oddities of humanity, I walk over to greet the colleagues exiting two newly arrived police cars.

"What do you need?" Sylvia asks before she's even out of the car. She's been on the force for four years already, but her chirpy enthusiasm has yet to wear off. There'd been a bet going when she first started working with us, on when she'd start showing up with the same distrustful and depressive face as the rest of us, but we'd all lost. Nobody had bet on more than two years, and her smile is still in place. Her platinum blonde hair is up in her usual simple ponytail, and her uniform fits a little looser than what most of the women choose. My guess is she's used to getting attention for her looks and has chosen a uniform hiding some of her forms on purpose.

"Thank you for coming, Sylvia," I say as I shake her hand. I point to the tarp. "The dead body's over there, but I'll ask Askild to take care of that part. From what I understand, our victim fell from the balcony up there." I point to the balcony on the third floor, with a door open and white curtains blowing out. There must be more wind up there than down here.

"I'd like for you to take your team and get into the apartment up there. Let me know what you find."

Sylvia gives me a huge smile. "Sure thing, boss." Then she waves for her colleagues to follow her before trotting up to the building's main entrance.

Askild and his team are already working on setting up a tent around the dead body. We don't always do this, but in an area this crowded, we want to minimize the impact of pictures ending up on the internet, and we want to work in peace.

Henrik, the guy in charge of managing and interrogating the crowd, comes over. He's a bit on the short side—his unruly dark blond hair only barely reaches past my shoulders—but excellent at this type of work. He has an eye for details and his bullshit meter is usually spot on.

"I have at least seven witnesses seeing the body hit the ground," he says. "He apparently screamed on his way down—but not before, from what I can gather—so that drew the attention of quite a few people. I also have a girl who claims she saw him going over the railing up there." He nods his head in the direction of a young girl, probably eighteen or so, who's sitting alone on a bench inside the secured perimeter, a melting ice cream long forgotten next to her.

Henrik flips open his notebook to check something, even though he's never forgotten a single detail from any crime scene he's ever worked on. "She says he came hopping out the balcony doors on one foot, arms flailing, then hit the rail with his hip, and toppled over."

I glance back up at the balcony. The railing doesn't appear particularly low. "How tall is our victim?"

Henrik shrugs. "Can't tell for sure, but I'm guessing close to two meters. That railing won't even have reached his hips."

I have a moment of compassion for our victim. Added to the discomfort of flying, here's yet another inconvenience to being tall. Balcony railings might not save you.

"She didn't see anybody else up there?" I ask.

"No. She did see the crab, though. Helped us find it."

"Ah. So we have our perpetrator already?"

Henrik cracks a smile. "He's even alive, if you want to interrogate him."

I chuckle and seriously consider doing just that when my radio crackles. "Boss," Sylvia says. "I think you should come up here."

I grab my radio as I march toward the building. "What did you find?"

"Uh." There's a moment of static. "When one person kills a lot of people, it's a mass murder. What is it when it's the other way around?"

"I'm not following."

"We have about fifty potential killers up here."

## 2

THE APARTMENT IS crawling with crabs. Literally. The type that's supposed to live in the ocean.

They cover the floor of the living room and the bedroom. The bathroom is clear, probably because the crabs prefer wooden floors to tiles. A couple have ventured across the threshold to the balcony and even as I watch, one passes through the railing and plummets down toward the street.

"Get that balcony closed," I snap. "We can't have crabs raining down on our colleagues working on the dead body below."

This case keeps getting weirder.

I step onto a chair to make sure I don't get attacked—those suckers can cut through shoes—and try to make sense of the situation.

Once the officers around me shut up, we're left listening to a chorus of crabs. You'd think they're silent creatures, but anyone who's ever cooked crabs knows better. Their sharp, pointy feet tapping on the container—or in this case floor—are complemented by the clicks of their claws as the creatures try to look menacing. Their little mouths open and close continually, making little bubbles which in turn burst in little *pops*.

"They haven't been here for long," I say. "They're still running all over the place with plenty of energy." Crabs can survive for quite some time out of water, but not indefinitely. If you buy live crabs, you try not to keep them alive for too long because otherwise it's just cruel. Too many hours in dry air, and they start gathering in groups, moving less, making less bubbles. This group can't be more than an hour or two out of the water.

Sylvie, standing on a kitchen chair next to me, meets my gaze. "Should we assume our victim wasn't the one to put them here?"

"I think that's a safe assumption. Do we know how they were transported here? Any crates lying around?"

"Nothing," Sylvie replies. "We checked the entire apartment. Seems like there's a girlfriend, by the way."

I nod. "Get someone to find the girlfriend. Have her brought to the police station. Search the area looking for crates. You don't transport crabs in just anything. Chances are, someone was walking around with at least two crates of live crabs not so long ago. I want witnesses and I want crates."

"Sure thing, boss," Sylvie says and jumps down from her chair to follow my orders.

I remain standing on my chair for several moments, looking down on the teeming crabs like a god, wondering if it's considered tampering with evidence if I bring one home to eat it.

The girlfriend is a little slip of a thing. She barely reaches my chest and I could probably lift her using just one arm.

Considering her boyfriend was even taller than me, they must have been quite a sight together.

Tears are falling down her cheeks at regular intervals, making straight tracks past her jaw, down her neck, and into her neckline. She's one of those women who manages to be beautiful even with eyes red from crying. The redness only enhances the turquoise of her eyes.

"When was the last time you saw your boyfriend?" I ask her. We've already been here for a while and are done with the preliminaries. We've also lost a good deal of time to crying, but that is to be expected.

"Last night," she answers. "Before he left for his shift at the hospital."

Our victim was a nurse at the Sankt Olav's hospital, specialized in pediatrics.

"We usually have dinner together," she continues between sobs. "He leaves a couple of hours before I go to bed. I have to leave around seven thirty in the morning, so we don't meet then when he's working night shifts."

I search for the right word to formulate my next question. "What state was the apartment in when you left?"

"State?" Her cute nose bunches into a frown and she lets out an uneven breath. "What do you mean, state? It was like it usually is. I might have left some dishes out and the hamper might be overflowing, but—"

I reach across the table separating us and place my hand on top of hers. "We're not judging you for the cleanliness of your apartment," I assure her. "Believe me, it looked just fine compared to the stuff I usually see." At least I thought it did. It was honestly a little difficult to remember because of all the crabs.

She shifts on her chair, as if searching for a more comfortable position. "Why are you asking, anyway? Is there something wrong with the apartment? Was there a break-in? Is that what happened?"

I decide she probably doesn't know about the crabs. "As far as we know, there was no break-in," I tell her. "But the place was crawling with crabs when we got there."

She shifts on her chair again and her eyes shoot up. "Crabs? As in *crabs* crabs?"

"As in the kind that's supposed to be in the ocean, yes. There were fifty of them."

Her mouth drops open. "In my apartment."

"Yes."

She jerks in her seat as if something suddenly bit her. She must have a wedgie; never fun when under close scrutiny.

I decide I've gotten everything I can from her and let her go home.

Hopefully, my colleagues have found and removed all the crabs by now.

## 4

Sylvia calls me while I'm having coffee. I'm in the district's top floor break room, which has an unimpeded view of a large intersection, the bus station, and the train station. It might inspire escape, but not much else.

"We found the crates," Sylvia says, and I can hear the smile in her voice. "Didn't have to go farther than the building's trash in the back."

"Do you think that means the person who brought the crabs in knew the building well?" I stare at the vending machine in front of me, eying a Snickers bar on the top shelf. It looks really tempting.

"Could be," Sylvie answers. "But the trash bins aren't exactly difficult to find once you go out the back door. It *does* mean that whoever brought the crabs probably left through the back. So, I'm thinking we won't have many witnesses."

I grunt in agreement.

"I found the vendor," Sylvia continues. "Name was on the crates, so we went down to the docks to check it out."

That sounded promising. I knock on the vending machine glass before turning my back on it. The way this case is going, I'm not going to have time to work out tonight, so it's difficult to justify the snack.

"The guy sold at least thirty crates of crabs this morning—seems like if you want fresh crab you have to be an early riser—and he claims not to be good with associating orders with faces. So we don't exactly have a list of suspects. But if we show him pictures, he should be able to say if he's seen the guy before, at least."

I stare out the window, watching as the bus from the airport spits out five travelers in front of the bus station. "Were they only guys? Or are you just saying guy by default?"

"Oh." Sylvia's voice is muffled while she talks to someone in the background. "Only guys," she confirms after a few seconds.

"At least that should rule out the girlfriend for good."

I end the call, but before I can leave the break room, I'm joined by Frank, our coroner.

"Frank," I say as I shake his hand. "Do you have any news for me on the crab case?" Inside I'm grinning, but I manage to keep a straight face. Frank has never been accused of having a sense of humor.

"I do," Frank says. He stops just inside the door, his white scrubs impeccably ironed, and his hair slicked to the side just so, not a single hair out of place. "The report is on your desk, but you told me to come find you when I was finished. I'm finished."

"Thank you, Frank. Would you mind giving me the highlights?" This exercise is always a bit tricky with Frank, but I figure he needs the exercise, and from time to time he makes an observation that nobody else would have made. It has even helped me solve a case or two.

Frank nods and keeps his eyes on my chest as he makes his report. "Cause of death was a fall from the third floor. Broke his neck and smashed his head in." His eyes flick up to mine to check my reaction.

"Okay. Go on."

Frank swallows but I know he's gained confidence from getting the right information in first.

"Only other contusion on his body is from the crab claw on his right big toe. Didn't smoke. Seems unlikely he was alcoholic. Had pubic lice and probably some STD. A mole on his leg should have been removed because it's not symmetrical. He—"

"Hang on," I interrupt. I know it's impolite, but once Frank gets going on his list of observations, it can take a while before he finishes. "How do you know he had an STD?"

Frank's gaze is locked on mine now, and I can see the annoyance at me not getting something that's obvious to him but isn't to me, but then it morphs into satisfaction at getting to explain it to me. "Because of the pubic lice," he says.

"Is that what it sounds like?"

"It's lice in the pubic hair," Frank says.

"And our victim had that?"

"No."

I fight to stay calm, and win. Having worked with Frank before has its advantages. "First you tell me he has lice, then you tell me he doesn't?"

"He doesn't have lice anymore because he doesn't have pubic hair anymore. He shaved it all off. Probably because of the lice."

Huh, this is actually starting to make some sort of sense. "Then how do you know he had them?"

"Because of the sores he got from scratching. Several were still fresh."

I'm very happy not to have to make that observation myself. "Are these pubic lice considered an STD, then?" I can't remember ever hearing anything about them.

"Technically, yes," Frank says. "Since they are transmitted through physical contact, they usually travel from one carrier to another during intimate contact. But they are often coupled with other STDs, so I've ordered a complete analysis."

I thank Frank for his work and let him return to his office in the cellar.

I turn my nose homeward, wondering if there could be any kind of connection between the pubic lice and the man's death.

Lice and crabs. What critter's up next?

## 5

I tell my wife Ingrid about the case over dinner. I know I'm not supposed to, but she can be trusted to keep her mouth shut and she's proved to be an effective sounding board over the years. Not to mention her expertise from reading innumerable mystery novels.

I'm happy to be able to tell her an original story, for once, and we're both grinning at each other over tonight's steak. When I finish recounting my talk with Frank, Ingrid stops, her fork halfway to her mouth.

"What?" I ask her. She has that look that means she's thought of something I haven't.

"He had *the crabs*." She says the word crab in English, as if that should mean something to me.

"No, he had lice," I tell her slowly. "Then someone put crabs in his apartment and he fell off his balcony as a result." I narrow my eyes and smile at her. "What am I not getting?"

"In English, these lice are called crabs," she explains. "Because they're shaped like crabs. Compared to the head lice, at least."

I drop my fork onto my plate, my food forgotten. "So there really is a link between the two critters!"

"I'd say there is." Ingrid takes a slow sip of her water as her eyes twinkle. "He probably gave someone *the crabs*, so they returned the favor!"

I'M BACK WITH the girlfriend. She appeared innocent during our first interview, but she'd also been moving around on her chair as if she'd been itching, and that makes her my prime suspect of our payback crime.

"How long have you had lice?" I ask her as soon as I've made sure everything we say is being recorded.

"What?" Her hand goes to her hair. "I've never had lice! Not even when I was a kid."

"I'm not talking about head lice," I tell her. I wait until she makes one of her little wiggles on her chair. "I'm talking pubic lice." Just to make sure she gets the point, I nod in direction of her crotch.

Seriously, the things I get to say on this case.

"I don't—" She wiggles again. And again. "But…" I can see the understanding dawning in her eyes, and the shame reddening her cheeks.

Dammit. If she's guilty, she's also the world's best actress.

"Can you tell me how long you've been itching like that?" I ask her. "I'm afraid it's important to the case."

Her cheeks stay beet red, but she seems to be thinking back. "Maybe a month? I'm sorry, but I can't be sure."

"That's fine," I tell her. "Now, I'm sorry to have to ask this. But do you think it's possible your boyfriend had a mistress?"

I watch her reaction closely. If she's not the one to accuse the man of giving her the crabs, it has to be someone outside of the couple.

Except only men had bought crabs that morning.

The mistress could have had an accomplice, maybe?

The woman's color had been returning to normal, but now it shoots back into red, this time in anger. "What kind of a question is that? He's *dead* and you try to sully his memory by accusing him of adultery?"

She shifts on her chair again.

*She* also has *the crabs*.

Could the crabs have been intended for *her*?

"Do *you* have a lover?" I ask her.

She goes even redder. It's covering her entire neck now. "What… How dare you? I would *never*… The very *idea*…"

I let her sputter. She *does* have a lover.

I work on her for almost an hour more, but she refuses to admit to adultery, nor give any names.

No matter. I'll find him.

I SPEND THE next two days interviewing the girlfriend's friends and colleagues.

Nobody admits to being the lover. Nobody thinks it's possible she had one. Why would she, when she had such a perfect relationship with our victim?

I realize that if I pretend to let the case go, and just rule it as a freak accident, the lover will probably prop up eventually, now that the boyfriend's out of the picture, but I want to *find* the man. I want to solve the case myself.

Once I've made my way through all the girlfriend's acquaintances, I get desperate and start in on the boyfriend's circle. It *is* possible she fell for one of his friends or colleagues, after all.

I'm at the pediatrics wing at the hospital, listening to the victim's colleagues singing his praises. He'd apparently been very well appreciated by everyone—at least, that's how they tell the story now he's dead.

"If he found the time," one of the nurses tells me, "he'd dress up like a clown and get the kids who needed it the most to laugh. There are professionals who do that, of course, but they can only come once a week. So he liked stepping in whenever he could." She puts on a dreamy smile. "The kids loved it."

I'm revisiting my conclusion of the girlfriend being the one to have a lover. This woman looks like she wouldn't have minded sharing a bed with her late colleague.

"We all loved it when he did the clown routine," the girl continues. "In fact, Tom even accompanied him a time or two. Didn't you, Tom?" She appeals to a tall dark-haired guy leaning against the wall. He hasn't said a word so far.

"Yes," he says. I expect him to go on, but he goes back to his silence.

"Tom is American," the gushy girl explains. "His Norwegian is getting quite good, but he prefers to practice with the kids. With us, he usually talks English."

I nod in understanding. As she goes back to talking about how wonderful a man the victim was, I tune her out. My eyes stay on the American.

My brain is trying to tell me something. I recognize the feeling, like there's this thought just out of reach, but I just know that if I can reach it, I'll solve the case.

"Have we met before?" I ask the man in English. His face seems sort of familiar, but he doesn't have any particular feature that draws the eye.

"I don't think so," he replies. "I've only been here for a couple of months."

The girl tries gushing about how good his Norwegian is despite being here for such a short time, but I hold up a hand so she'll shut up. It works.

"I'm pretty sure I've seen you before," I tell the guy. But there was something different, something that draws the eye, but which isn't there right now.

Maybe it's the clothes? He's wearing scrubs at work, but if I'd seen him out and about, he'd have worn something like jeans…a t-shirt? I try to visualize it.

The guy scratching his crotch when we were securing the crime scene.

He's *American*. He'd know the expression *the crabs*, unlike most Norwegians, who, like me, associate that word solely with the creatures in the ocean which are so delicious to eat.

I'm too caught up in the moment to think before I act. I point at the guy. "You have the crabs!"

He shoots away from the wall, straightening to his full height. "I do not!"

"Can you prove that?"

Though I'm not a fan of what I had to see after asking my question, it did resolve the case.

The American didn't have the crabs because he'd shaved it all off, just like our victim. And just like our victim, he had the sores and an accompanying less fun STD.

Once we showed his picture to the guy selling the crabs, the case was a wrap.

The crabs *had* been intended for our victim. He *did* have an affair, it just wasn't with a woman.

Of course, the lice hadn't turned up out of nowhere. Turns out I was right about the girlfriend, and once the American was arrested for unintentionally causing his lover's death, she started openly dating one of her colleagues.

Said colleague had a reputation for frequently touching his crotch, a habit he suddenly got rid of when he got a girlfriend.

Or rather, when said girlfriend explained about the crabs.

# THANK YOU

THANK YOU FOR reading *Critters*. I hope you enjoyed it!

Since I'm a Norwegian living in France, most of my stories take place in one of the two countries. For this one, I clearly wanted to take a quick trip home, and had probably eaten crab not too long ago. Unfortunately, I can't quite remember where the idea of the twist with the other type of crab came from...

If you liked the story, you might want to check out some of my other books mentioned on the next page. It's mostly Mysteries, but a few Science Fiction short stories will pop up, too.

And don't forget that the first book of my *Tolosa Mystery* series, *The Red Brick Haze*, is available for free on my website.

*R.W. Wallace*
www.rwwallace.com

## Also by R.W. Wallace

### Mystery

#### The Tolosa Mystery Series
*The Red Brick Haze* (free)
*The Red Brick Cellars*
*The Red Brick Basilica*

#### Ghost Detective Shorts (coming soon)
*Just Desserts*
*Lost Friends*
*Family Bonds*
*Till Death*
*Family History*
*Common Ground*
*Heritage*
*Eternal Bond*
*New Beginnings*

#### Short Stories
*Cold Blue Eternity*
*Hidden Horrors*
*Critters*
*Gertrude and the Trojan Horse*
*First Impressions*
*Let Them Eat Cake*
*Out of Sight*
*Two's Company*
*Like Mother Like Daughter*

## Fantasy (short stories)
*Unexpected Consequences*
*Morbier Impossible*
*A Second Chance*

## Science Fiction (short stories)
*The Vanguard*

### Lollapalooza Shorts
*Quarantine*
*Common Enemies*
*Coiled Danger*
*Mars Meeting*

## Adventure (short stories)
*Size Matters*

# ABOUT THE AUTHOR

R.W. WALLACE WRITES in most genres, though she tends to end up in mystery more often than not. Dead bodies keep popping up all over the place whenever she sits down in front of her keyboard.

The stories mostly take place in Norway or France; the country she was born in and the one that has been her home for two decades. Don't ask her why she writes in English—she won't have a sensible answer for you.

Her Ghost Detective short story series appears in *Pulphouse Magazine*, starting in issue #9.

You can find all her books, long and short, all genres, on rwwallace.com.

www.ingramcontent.com/pod-product-compliance
Lightning Source LLC
LaVergne TN
LVHW041601070526
838199LV00046B/2083